Red Riding Hood
Meets
the Three Bears

written by Charlotte Guillain
illustrated by Karl West

capstone

2

One sunny morning, Little Red Riding Hood packed up a basket of cupcakes and left to visit her grandma.

"Stay on the path, and don't go off into the woods," her mom warned. "The Big Bad Wolf lives there."

"I will," said Little Red Riding Hood.

But the path was **overgrown**, and soon Little Red Riding Hood was lost! She didn't notice Goldilocks walking in the other direction.

The Big Bad Wolf was happy. "Two little girls lost in the woods," he muttered with a **sly** grin. "More *food for me.*"

Then he went after Goldilocks.

Little Red Riding Hood finally arrived at a small cottage.

"Oh!" she **gasped**. "That's strange. I thought Grandma lived in a blue house. Maybe she painted it."

The door was open. Little Red Riding Hood went inside.

"Grandma!" she called. "Where are you?"

8

"Three bowls of porridge!" said Little Red Riding Hood. "What a big breakfast you have, Grandma!"

Little Red Riding Hood cleaned up and put away the bowls of porridge. Then she got out her cupcakes and put them on a plate.

"Grandma!" she called. "Where are you?"

Little Red Riding Hood went to look in the living room.

"What big chairs you have, Grandma!" she said.

It was strange. Grandma had painted the house and bought three new chairs.

Little Red Riding Hood looked all around for her grandma.

"Grandma!" she called. "Where are you?"

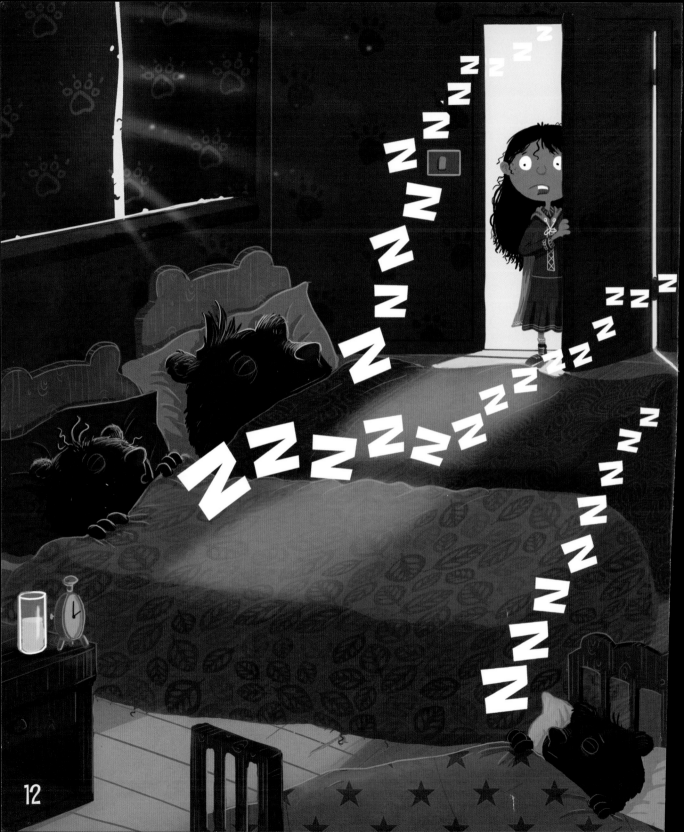

Then Little Red Riding Hood went upstairs to see if Grandma was taking a nap.

She opened the door and looked inside the bedroom. She saw three new beds!

"My, what a loud snore you have, Grandma!" said Little Red Riding Hood.

She turned on the light and shouted, "Wake up!"

ZZZZZZZ

The three bears woke up.

Little Red Riding Hood screamed and ran downstairs. The three bears ran after her.

"Don't be scared!" called Mother Bear.

"Cupcakes!" said Baby Bear when he saw the plate on the table.

"They are *for* my grandma," said Little Red Riding Hood.

"You've come to the wrong house," said Father Bear.

The three bears took Little Red Riding Hood through the woods to her grandma's house.

But when they arrived, Little Red Riding Hood **gasped**, "Oh no!"

The Big Bad Wolf was about to eat Grandma and Goldilocks!

Just then, the three bears gave a great big ...

... rOAR!

The Big Bad Wolf screamed and ran away.

"Well," said Grandma, "that was a strange day."

"At least we still have the cupcakes," said Little Red Riding Hood.

"Then let's finish the day with a tea party," said Grandma.

And that's what they did.

Little Red Riding Hood

Little Red Riding Hood was first written down by the Brothers Grimm. They lived in Germany 200 years ago. They called the story *Little Red-Cap*. Little Red-Cap is going to visit her grandmother and meets a wolf on the way. The wolf goes ahead to Grandmother's house and eats her! The wolf then puts on Grandmother's clothes and waits for Little Red-Cap. When she arrives, the wolf eats her too! Luckily a hunter cuts Little Red-Cap and Grandmother out of the wolf's stomach.

Goldilocks and the Three Bears

Goldilocks is a traditional British story. When it was first written down, it was called *The Story of the Three Bears*. It is about an old woman who goes into the three bears' house. She eats the baby bear's porridge, breaks his chair, and sleeps in his bed. When the bears come back and wake her up, she runs away.

Glossary

gasp—to breathe in quickly in surprise

overgrown—covered with plants and weeds

sly—secretive and cunning

Writing Prompts

If you could be a character in this story, who would you choose? Why?

Imagine you are Baby Bear. Write a letter to Little Red Riding Hood to say thank you for the tea party.

Write some instructions for other children going through the woods to visit Grandma. How can they stay safe?

Read More

Gunderson, Jessica. *Little Red Riding Hood: Stories Around the World* (Multicultural Fairy Tales). North Mankato, Minnesota: Picture Window Books, 2014

Rojankovsky, F. *The Three Bears*. New York: Little Golden Books, 2012

Rosen Schwartz, Corey. *Ninja Red Riding Hood*. New York: G.P. Putnam's Sons, 2014

Willems, Mo. *Goldilocks and the Three Dinosaurs*. New York: Balzer & Bray, 2012

Internet sites

Facthound offers a safe, fun way to find web sites related to this book. All the sites on Facthound have been researched by our staff.

Here's all you do:
Visit **www.facthound.com**
Type in this code: 9781410983046

Read all the books in the series:

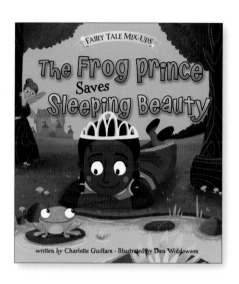

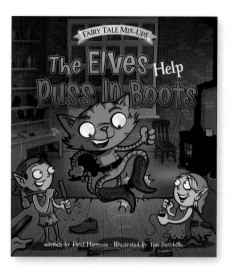

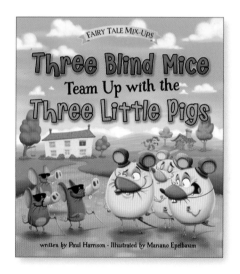

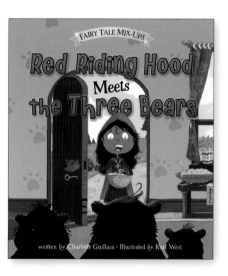

Visit www.mycapstone.com

© 2017 Raintree
an imprint of Capstone Global Library, LLC
Chicago, Illinois

To contact Capstone Global Library please call 800-747-4992, or visit our website www.capstonepub.com

Edited by Penny West
Designed by Steve Mead
Original illustrations © Capstone Global Library Ltd 2016
Illustrated by Karl West, Astound US
Production by Steve Walker
Originated by Capstone Global Library Limited

20 19 18 17 16
10 9 8 7 6 5 4 3 2 1

Library of Congress Cataloging-in-Publication data is available on the Library of Congress website.

ISBN: 978-1-4109-8304-6 (library binding)
ISBN: 978-1-4109-8312-1 (paperback)
ISBN: 978-1-4109-8316-9 (eBook PDF)

Summary: Little Red Riding Hood is lost in the woods. She thinks she's found her grandma's house, but why is there three of everything inside?

Printed and bound in China
PO007731LEOF16